To my dad
who has been up in the sky
for a long, long time.
To all the dads in the sky,
seas, and cherry trees.

I would also like to thank
very, very much, in order of
arrival and not importance:
the beginning of healing,
Mino, David, Lucia,
Giampaola, Milena, Elena,
Debbie, Claudia and a lion...
                            —VF

Vittoria Facchini
was born in Molfetta,
Puglia, in the south of Italy.
She studied graphic design
in Florence and discovered
illustration quite unexpectedly
while in Venice, and fell in love.
Vittoria has created many
books, but this is her first to
be published in the US,
where it makes its debut.

First published in 2017 by Enchanted Lion Books,
67 West Street, 317A, Brooklyn, New York 11222
Copyright © 2017 by Vittoria Facchini for the text and illustrations
Published by arrangement with Debbie Bibo Agency
English-language translation copyright © 2017 by Anna Celada
Design & layout: Duška Karanov
All rights reserved under International
and Pan-American Copyright Conventions
A CIP record is on file with the Library of Congress
ISBN: 978-1-59270-222-0
Printed in Italy by Grafiche AZ

First Printing

5 CHERRIES

Vittoria Facchini

Translated from the Italian by Anna Celada

ENCHANTED LION BOOKS

NEW YORK

Children, look! Aren't they beautiful?
The first spring cherries from your father's tree.

5 for you, and 5 for you. Here, take them.

But Mom, just these? So few?
What am I gonna do with only 5 cherries?
Nothing.

Thanks, Mom, all these? So many?
I'm gonna do a ton of things with these 5 cherries.
I'll play loads of games!

I'm gonna eat them all at once!

I'm just gonna look at mine, they're so pretty.

I'll make a healing medicine for my sick little patients.

And I'll teach my dog to be patient!

I'll be a jester! And I'll do a jiggety-jester-jig.

I'll share mine with my friends.
Everything's ready. They're coming to tea.

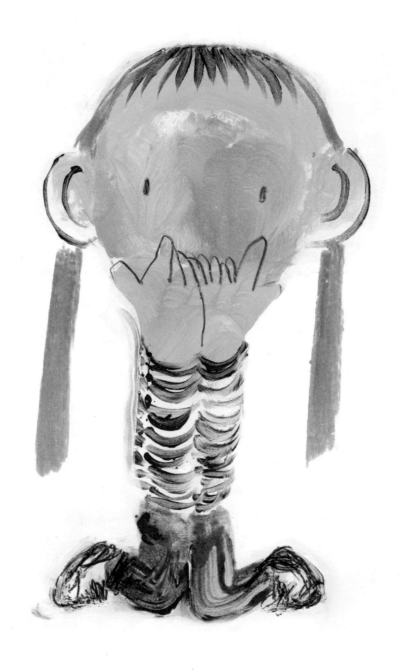

That's it. I'm not playing anymore.
There just aren't enough cherries.

Here, take mine. Is that better?
Come on, let's keep playing...

My cherries were cursed and I ate them.
I slept and slept for more than 100 years.

Then you were awakened with a kiss.

No, yuck! Never!
I just woke up without a kiss.

Hey, guess which hand has the cherry.
Bet you guess wrong and I win all your cherries.

I'm gonna go ready, aim, fire!
I'll bother you and make you mad.

I'll do a rain dance to help this struggling little tree bloom.

I'll give my super cannons super cherry ammunition!

And I'll make a super cherry pie. Just like Mom!

I'll make a bunch of flowers.
It's called a bouquet!

Hey! Look at me!

What for?

I've made medals for my general's uniform.

I'll make cherry-red lipstick that will sparkle on my lips and face.

Look!

I'll cook yummy foods and soups for my hungry little creatures.
Some for you, some for you, some for you... and there's lots more too!

Hey, look what I did!

Now I forgot what I was thinking.

I'll take my cherries to the beach and we'll sit really, really still and listen to the vastness of the ocean.

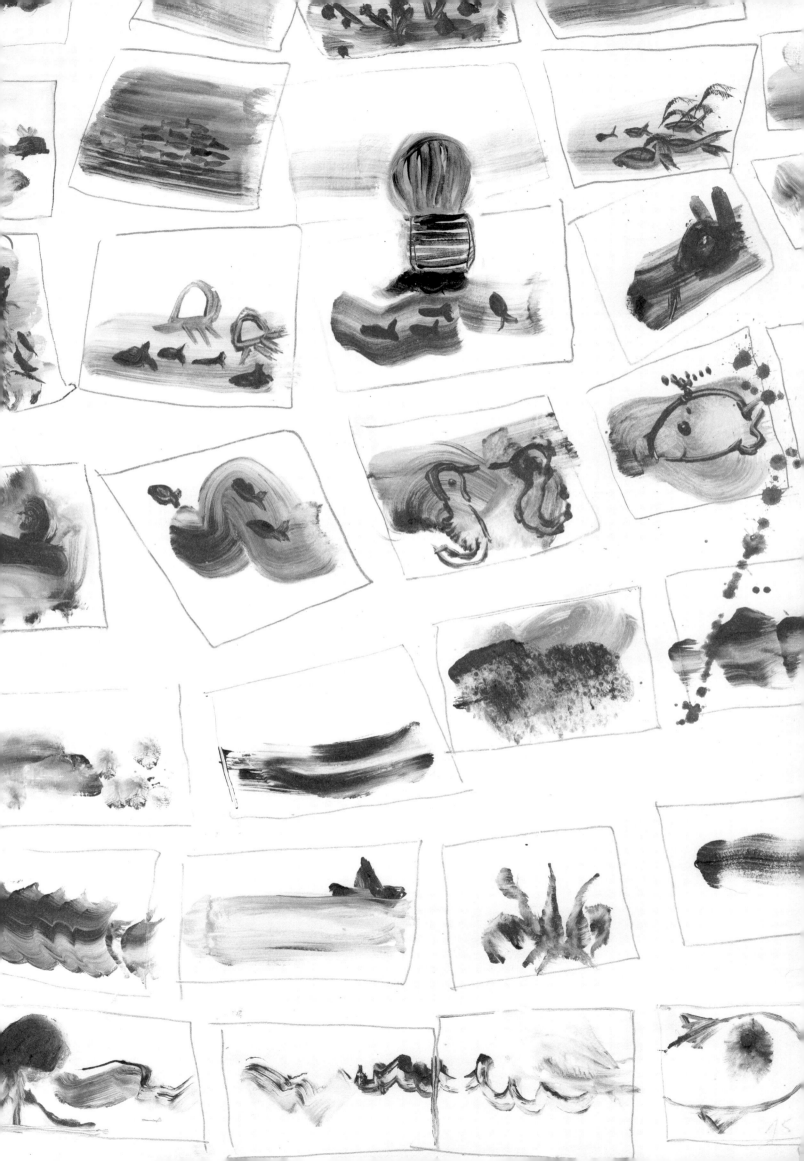

I will—no, we will protect them.

They rain down from the sky.
They fall down on the ground.
They are everywhere, destroying everything.
It is the war...
And I am just a child...

No, there isn't any war. I'm gonna lay mine gently on the ground.

I'll put mine on a piece of paper and make a drawing with special cherry-effects!

I'll make a perfect cherry circle.

Perfect?

Yes, perfect.

I'm gonna throw mine way up high, so Dad can see them and touch them and eat them too.

But that's too high. You can't do it.

Yes, I can. Just watch me!

I'm gonna plant a secret garden.
In one little seed, there's already an orchard.

I'll be a fool clowning around.

And I'll make mom smile when I fool around!

I'll make a special braid that I'll toss down, down, down...

And I'll do a special trick that goes up, up, up...

I'm gonna sell mine at a fruit stand.

How much will you sell them for?

13, 86, 94, 11 thousand a pound.

Seriously? That's way too much.

What? That's not expensive at all!

I'm gonna paint them from real life. That way I'll really see them.

I'll blow kisses with mine.

I'll make weird things as presents.

Children? Where are you?
Time to go!

Hooray! Coming, Mom!
But what about the 5 cherries?
Want some? Maybe we can eat them.

Already, Mom?
Do we really have to go?
I wish we didn't have to...

Give me 5 more minutes, Mom.

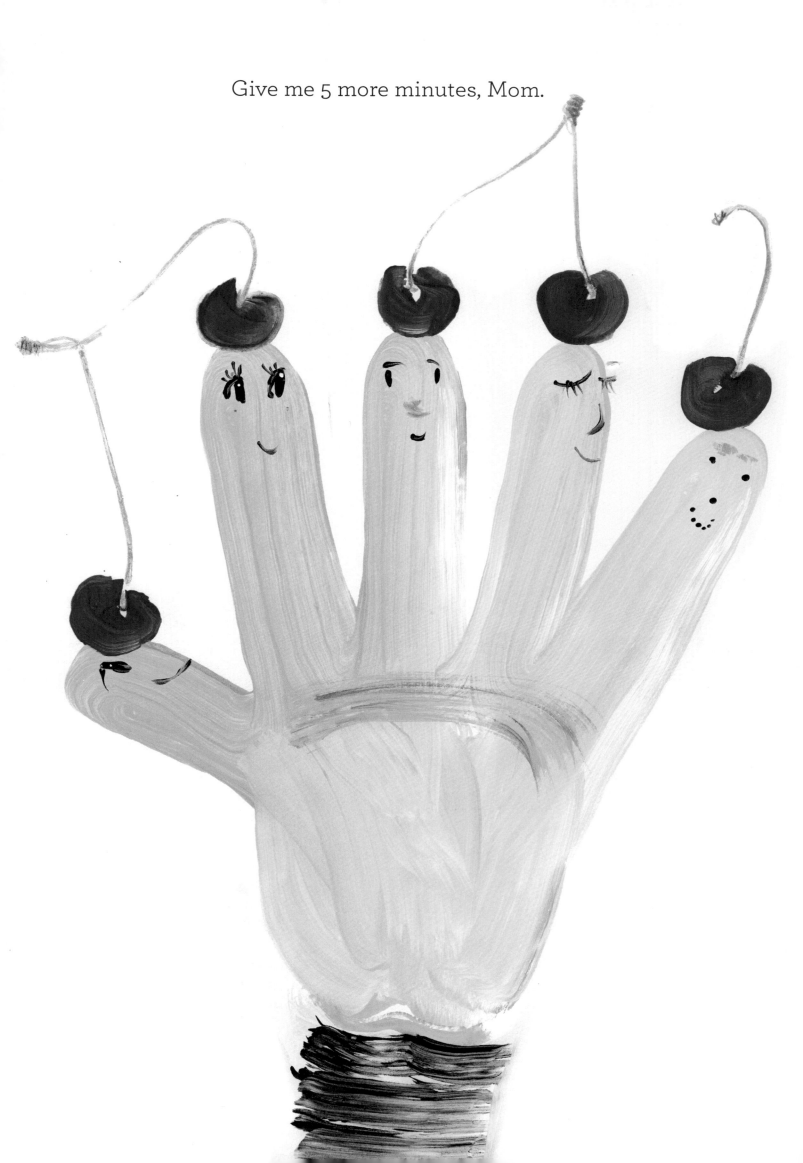

Just 5 more.